THREE
LITTLE KITTENS

Illustrated by MASHA

A GOLDEN BOOK • NEW YORK

THE LITTLE GOLDEN BOOKS
ARE PREPARED UNDER THE SUPERVISION OF
MARY REED, Ph.D.
ASSISTANT PROFESSOR OF EDUCATION
TEACHERS COLLEGE, COLUMBIA UNIVERSITY

A COMMEMORATIVE FACSIMILE EDITION PUBLISHED ON THE OCCASION OF
THE 50TH ANNIVERSARY OF LITTLE GOLDEN BOOKS

to Albert

The three little kittens—

they lost their mittens,

And they began to cry,

"Oh! Mother dear,

We sadly fear,

Our mittens we have lost!"

"What! lost your mittens,
You naughty kittens?
Then you shall have no pie."

"Meow, meow, meow, meow,

Meow, meow, meow, meow."

The three little kittens—
they found their mittens,

And they began to cry,
"Oh! Mother dear,

See here, see here,
Our mittens we have found."

"What! found your mittens,
You good little kittens?
Then you shall have some pie."

"Purr, purr, purr, purr,

Purr, purr, purr, purr."

The three little kittens
put on their mittens,
And soon ate up the pie;

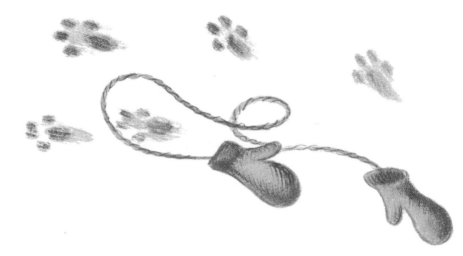

"Oh! Mother dear,

We greatly fear,

Our mittens we have soiled."

"What! soiled your mittens?
You naughty kittens!"

Then they began to sigh,
"Meow, meow, meow, meow,
Meow, meow, meow, meow."

The three little kittens—

they washed their mittens,

And hung them up to dry;

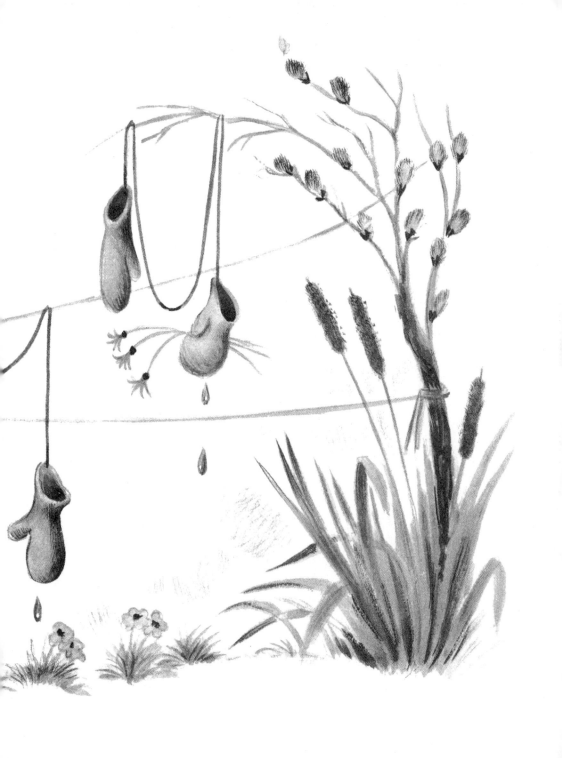

THE STORM

"Oh! Mother dear,
    Look here, look here,
    Our mittens we have washed."

"What! washed your mittens?

You darling kittens!

But I smell a rat close by!
Hush! hush!"

"Meow, meow,

Meow, meow, meow, meow."